Graceland Cemetery in Chicago

A Sherlockian Walk Midst the Tombstones

Author and tour guide
Brenda Rossini

ePub ISBN 978-1-78705-057-0
PDF ISBN 978-1-78705-058-7
Paperback 978-1-78705-056-3

Published in the UK by MX Publishing
335 Princess Park Manor, Royal Drive,
London, N11 3GX

www.mxpublishing.com

Cover design by Brian Belanger

DEDICATION

To My Sherlockian Friends Past and Present

Graceland Cemetery
A SHERLOCKIAN WALK MIDST THE TOMBSTONES
Brenda Rossini, Author and tour guide

Do not go gentle into that good night,

Old age should burn and rave at close of day;

Rage, rage against the dying of the light.

Dylan Thomas

GRACELAND: founded in 1860 upon 80 acres. Père Lachaise cemetery in Paris is 110 Acres. [SEP]Graceland was built outside of the city because the Chicago Fire Dept. had health and safety concerns about shallow graves and cholera affecting water supply.

To the east, along the cemetery, the El train was erected, going south and north, bringing mourners to the gravesites with ease.

HERE DWELL ETERNALLY famous Chicagoans, from Indian fighters to Chicago politicians to veterans of foreign wars, boxers, civil rightists, and doomed victims. Farewell requiems are marked on stone and marble tombstones, mausoleums, and obelisks.

Among the many monument inscriptions, the wanderer will recognize Chicago streets and schools: Kinzie, Honore, Washburne, Larrabee, Loomis, Kimball, Whipple, Altgeld, Carpenter, Sherman.

Among the principal sculptors, but buried elsewhere, is Lorado Taft (1860-1936)—a famous "Prairie State" sculptor. He hired a team of women to assist with his sculptures--a team he called his "White Rabbits."

Taft's "Blackhawk Indian" statue stands in Oregon, Illinois. "Lincoln the Lawyer" is in Champaign/ , Illinois. "Fountain of Time" is at the Midway Pleasance near the University of Chicago leaving this magnificent architectural footprint in 1920. "Fountain of the Great Lakes" sits at the Art Institute.

"There's an east wind coming all the same, such a wind as never blew...It will be cold and bitter, Watson, and a good many of us may wither before its blast. But it's God's own wind none the less."

His Last Bow

PROCEED EAST FROM THE GRACELAND OFFICE AND ADJACENT PARKING (All Graceland lanes have names)

at right, the hooded shroud, black granite, "Eternal Silence," designed in 1909 by Lorado Taft. The dead man, Dexter Graves, was an early settler and filthy-rich hotelier who died in 1845. Looking into the shroud should give one an insight into death and forever silence. Other Taft sculptures will follow, including a Christian knight in armor.

To the left of Graves' Eternal Silence:

JOHN KINZIE, 1753 –1828, Chicago's first permanent white settler, first murderer, and the oldest gravestone here. There's a street named for him behind Marina City Towers which two pizza-like columns sit on the river at State Street. A native of Quebec and a fur trapper, Kinzie came to Chicago in 1804, settled in the homestead that Chicago's first impermanent, non-white settler, Jean Baptiste du Sable, built among the local natives. Du Sable was possibly the son of a pirate and a freed slave; he spoke French from either Haiti or Canada.

Kinzie murder lore

Kinzie was a real estate wheeler-dealer while living in Chicago. Jean La Lime, another trader and settler, likewise moved from Quebec to Chicago in 1792 and purchased a farm from du Sable. La Lime worked as an interpreter for Indians and traders at Fort Dearborn. On Feb. 17, 1812, La Lime and Kinzie fought and Kinzie stabbed La Lime to death. Kinzie fled north to Milwaukee. At the inquest, presided over by a fellow real estate patron, Kinzie claimed self-defense and that La Lime had fired a gun. Kinzie's motive may have been intentional. He may have killed La Lime to silence him about Kinzie's fur trade profiteering. Kinzie was exonerated and lived another 16 years in Chicago, even serving as justice of the peace.

Kinzie was buried in Graceland Cemetery but La Lime was forgotten until his coffin was unearthed near St. James Church on Rush Street; his bones are preserved at the Chicago Historical Society. note Shakespeare's epitaph: *"Blessed be the man that spares these stones, And cursed be he that moves my bones."*

SHERLOCKIAN NOTE: In Arthur Conan Doyle's (1859-1930) *Valley of Fear* and *Study in Scarlet*, the mysteries perceptively follow lawlessness and corruption —the inclinations of men seeking fortunes in the wild lands of North America. In other *Adventures,* men return rough but rich from gold mines in South Africa, South America and Australia.

NORTH ON CENTER LANE TO CHAPEL BUILDING

Right

JOHN JONES (1816-1879)--First black man to gain prominence in Cook County. Son of a free mulatto woman and a German (Bromfield). Jones married Mary Richardson, herself a free woman. The couple moved to Chicago. He started a tailoring business, struggling to prove he was a free man. Their house was on Dearborn St. where abolitionists met, including Alan Pinkerton and the early American suffragettes. He was elected a Chicago commissioner after the Chicago Fire.

Left

CHIEF JUSTICE, U.S. SUPREME COURT, MELVILLE FULLER, 1888-1910. He had one year of legal training, at Harvard, in a day when legal apprenticeship was customary. His tenure at the Supreme Court is remembered for the 1896 decision *Plessy v. Ferguson.* In Louisiana, shoemaker Homer Plessy, a 1/8 black man (under law, a Negro) refused

11

to leave his train seat among white passengers for the "colored" section. Plessy was convicted and sentenced to $20 or 20 days in jail. He appealed, eventually appearing before the Supremes where Fuller ruled with a 7-1 majority (John Marshall Harlan dissenting) that a "separate but equal" arrangement was constitutional. The decision inspired racially discriminatory laws for years until overruled in the 1954 Supreme Court decision, *Brown v. Board of Education.*

Another key decision in Fuller's Supreme Court was *Lochner v. New York*, a 1905 federal appeal filed by bakery owner Joseph Lochner. Fuller voted with the court's 6-3 majority to overturn a NY law which had barred bakeries from assigning employees to work in excess of 60 hours/week. During the 1930s Great Depression, *Lochner* provided the basis for the Supreme Court to invalidate pieces of Pres. Franklin D. Roosevelt's New Deal.

Justice Fuller was the granduncle of futurist and engineer Buckminster Fuller, who lived in a geodesic dome/house on Forest St. in Carbondale IL while he taught at Southern Illinois University, 1961-1971.

SHERLOCKIAN NOTE: Bucky Fuller was best friends with Samuel Rosenberg, author of the aptly-named *Naked is the Best Disguise: Death and Resurrection of Sherlock Holmes* (1974) in which the curious reader will find allusions to sexual expressions in the Holmes *Canon.* Sam also pilgrimaged to Meiringen in 1954 following publication of Dr. Philip Hench's journals of the Reichenbach Falls.

NAKED IS THE BEST DISGUISE

The Death & Resurrection
of Sherlock Holmes

Samuel Rosenberg

NORTH ALONGSIDE THE LANE PARALLEL AND WEST OF THE CHAPEL

at Right

ALLAN PINKERTON, founder of Pinkerton's detective agency and a bodyguard for Abraham Lincoln. Beside him lies Pinkerton employee, Kate Warne, the first female detective in the U.S. and a Union spy during the Civil War. Warne posed as a rich Southern belle to help Pinkerton uncover a poisoning plot against Abraham Lincoln by Baltimore secessionists. She posed as a fortune teller, among other costumes and ruses. Another Pinkerton detective lying in repose is Timothy Webster, hung as a spy by Confederates. Another Pinkerton was shot in the back while pursuing Jesse James.

Why are they all buried together? For those who came to Chicago, alone, to make a living, and with no family, the people with whom they worked became family.

SHERLOCKIAN NOTE: Who were two Pinkertons mentioned in the Canon?

James McParland in *Valley of Fear* infiltrated the Molly Maguires in the eastern coal fields.

Leverton is "the hero of the Long Island cave mystery" in *The Red Circle*.

Up the street, west by a few feet from the Pinkerton site

WILLIAM HULBERT (1832-1882)--founder of the National League of Professional Baseball Clubs. His grave is marked with a big baseball. Does he hear the crowd at Wrigley Field-- Cubs Park?

SHERLOCKIAN NOTE: Conan Doyle, a lifelong sportsman, was an avid fan and promoter of America's pastime of baseball. He was introduced to major league baseball on the second of his four trips to North America, between 1894 and 1924. Doyle thought it a better game than cricket and baseball players far fitter.

BASEBALL AND BOXING: A baseball held in a private antique collection, is one signed by Conan Doyle, Babe Ruth, the first black heavyweight champion Jack Johnson, and Clarence Darrow (who represented Leopold and Loeb...see Matt Rizzo gravesite, below).

East and back to the Pinkerton site and to its Left

Hoyt: 5 grave markers

A family killed Dec. 30,1903 in downtown Chicago's Iroquois Theatre fire: Emilie, adult daughter of grocer William Hoyt, and her three children, 15, 12 and 9. They died piled behind locked fire doors (among 600 deaths.) Emilie's husband, Frederick Morton Fox, son of a wealthy banking family, died 2 months later, never having recovered from the shock.

SHERLOCKIAN NOTE: In *Scandal in Bohemia*, Sherlock Holmes directs Watson to throw into an open window an incendiary "plumber's smoke rocket," immediately after which Holmes shouts an alarm of "Fire!" The Great Detective used the same ploy in the house of *the Norwood Builder*. Holmes' motivation may have been diverting, but Judge Oliver Wendell Holmes, Sherlock's namesake, would have determined his conduct reckless and criminally actionable—"a clear and present danger."

SOUTH TO CHAPEL, ON GREENWOOD TOWARDS SOUTH CORNER

Vincent Starrett's *221B*

Here dwell together still two men of note

Who never lived and so can never die:

How very near they seem, yet how remote

That age before the world went all awry.

But still the game's afoot for those with ears

Attuned to catch the distant view-halloo:

England is England yet, for all our fears—

Only those things the heart believes are true.

A yellow fog swirls past the window-pane

As night descends upon this fabled street:

A lonely hansom splashes through the rain,

The ghostly gas lamps fail at twenty feet.

Here, though the world explode, these two survive,

And it is always eighteen ninety-five.

VINCENT STARRETT (1886-1974) *Chicago Tribune* and *Daily News* columnist; Baker Street Irregulars cofounder; literary man of short stories, pulp, book reviews, children's books and detective yarns, including a series with fictional Chicago detective Jimmy Lavender, named after a Chicago Cubs baseball pitcher of the 1910s. He wrote *The Unique Hamlet: A Hitherto Unchronicled Adventure of Mr. Sherlock Holmes* and the imaginary biography *The Private Life of Sherlock Holmes* in 1933.

When Starrett died in 1974, he was without funds and a friend paid for his funeral. His grave, next to his wife, Ray, remained unmarked. On his 100th birthday, Oct. 26, 1986, his friends and Sherlockian fans joined together to erect this Bookman's headstone with the words: "*What would we do without books—old books. It is raining tonight, a bit beastly and coldly—with an odd quality of permanence in its sound—as if it had been raining just this way since the beginning of things—and would continue to rain just so until the end. And I have about a thousand books breathing around me in this cheerful room, and I don't care a damn.*"

AT GREENWOOD/MAIN AND A LINE OF MAUSOLEUMS

TURN L on MAIN, GOING NORTH

at Left

BOXER JACK JOHNSON, 1878–1946, the first black boxer to win World Heavyweight championship. He knocked out James Jeffries, the "Great White Hope," and incurred further wrath when he married white women. He fought and beat Oscar Wilde's nephew, Arthur Craven---who was looking for a financial score in the U.S. Jack Johnson was unapologetically provocative in his boxing career and life but retirement found him in obscurity. Miles Davis wrote a trumpet tribute in remembrance, and written on the record jacket sleeve: "Jack Johnson portrayed Freedom--it rang just as loud as it proclaimed him Champion." Other than a large stone with his surname, his Graceland grave is unmarked. See Ken Burns' 2005 film "Unforgivable Blackness: The Rise and Fall of Jack Johnson" and James Earl Jones in "The Great White Hope."

SHERLOCKIAN NOTE: Conan Doyle was a boxing fan. Sherlock Holmes was a bare-knuckled boxer. Doyle was asked to referee the 1910 fight between Jack Johnson and James Jeffries but declined because it was likely to foster bigotry. Conan Doyle wrote the *Adventure of the Three Gables* in 1926 in which a black boxer is described as having "a smoldering gleam of malice."

STRAIGHT TO BIG CLUMP OF BIGSHOTS

The tall pillar

GEORGE PULLMAN, 1831-1897, he of the eponymous trains and sleeping cars. Pullman was a strike-buster and so despised that his family buried him in a lead-lined coffin, encased in concrete, covered with steel railroad ties and then more concrete to keep it from being desecrated. A Corinthian column with seats around the base sits above. His industrial town of Pullman, built in 1886 for the workers, lies on the far southeast side of Chicago. In the 1894 Depression, Pullman had to trim his payroll--but refused to lower rents or prices. Trapped between lower wages and increasing debt, workers went on strike. Violence broke out and federal troops were brought in. The strike was broken. Gov. Altgeld also buried at Graceland, supported the strikers and was called an anarchist; his political career was finished. Pullman's employees had to return to work. The town of Pullman and its well-constructed residences are still occupied. The general area is contaminated some miles off from a huge landfill and steel mill rubbish (thank Chicago politicians who made big money). Lakeside, there is a now-enclosed, no-trespassing area, where people once picnicked and hiked, but control of which has been assumed by the U.S. government.

SHERLOCKIAN NOTE: *The Valley of Fear* (1913) was inspired by Conan Doyle's sympathy for Irish-American labor strikers, the Molly Maguires, in 1876 Pennsylvania. 20 Irishmen were hanged in the coal-producing area, based on the testimony of an undercover Pinkerton agent.

across

PETER SCHOENHOFEN (1827-1893) a brewer who opened shop in 1862 at Canalport and 18th St....future White Sox baseball park and Mayor Daley country. The main beer was Edelweiss. Recall that Holmes and Watson drank a beer at the Alpha Inn in *Blue Carbuncle*. Prohibition closed the brewery from 1920 to 1933. The tombstone is an unlikely combination of an Egyptian pyramid and sphinx with a Victorian-era angel, the dead man hedging his bets on an afterlife: *Prosit, Herr Schoenhofen.*

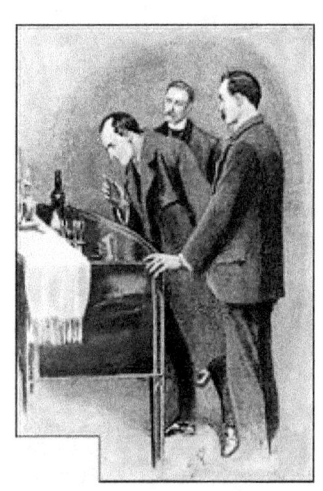

WILLIAM KIMBALL-1828-1904, piano and organ maker. White corinthian (slender and fluted) columns and an angel decorate his tomb. No pianos in Sherlock Holmes; he preferred the violin.

Across from Kimball

POTTER PALMER, 1826-1902. His and wife Bertha Honore's house on north Lake Shore Drive was a castle as is their home in Eternal Rest: a Greek temple with canopy atop a hill. He owned a dry goods store on old State St. (sold it to Marshall Field) and allowed customers to charge. He began developing State St. after the Great Fire of 1871. He built mansions in the Gold Coast area, along Lake Shore Drive, north to Oak St. He filled swamp land with sand from Lake Michigan and sold lots to his rich friends--hence "Gold Coast." There's also his Palmer House Hotel. "We didn't have much taste, but we had a lot of money," so say their gravesites. Bertha's family, the Honores, were also real estate magnates. Bertha retired to Sarasota, Florida; her children followed and there they established a sunny life of wealth and more real estate.

SHERLOCKIAN NOTE: Those of you who winter in Florida, be sure to look up the local Sarasota/Bradenton/St. Petersburg Sherlock Holmes society: Pleasant Places of Florida.

Larry Millett, prolific Sherlock Holmes pastiche author, in *the Ice Palace Murders* has Holmes and Watson staying at the Palmer House during a Chicago visit in 1896 to investigate a Palmer family murder.

MARTIN RYERSON(1818-1887) steel tycoon. Egyptian motif on the tomb. It was in fashion— perhaps the pharaonic echo of reincarnation.

SHERLOCKIAN NOTE: Conan Doyle's epitaph: *"Blade straight/Steel true."*

ALEXANDER C. McCLURG, bookseller and an American publisher of Conan Doyle. Also a Civil War general and military adviser. McClurg Court Apartments, east of Michigan Ave., are named for him, as is the bookstore at the Newberry Library.

The big tomb bed on the right

CHARLES WACKER, 1856-1929. He was a city planner. Wacker Drive along the Chicago River leads from the Ogilvie/Metra train station east to Michigan Avenue. His was a brewing family which advanced the technology of refrigeration. The family lived in Old Town and in Lake Forest for its stables. One set of descendants lies buried near the Lake Forest beachfront. A still-living Wacker operates Green Bay stables in Cape Town, South Africa (Green Bay is a road that runs north and south along the north shore of Lake Michigan in Illinois.). The horsey set was big in the north shore. There are vividly brutal stories associated with these ostler cliques.

SHERLOCKIAN NOTE: Conan Doyle was a lover of horses and stocked them at his homes. He also wrote horse poetry. Most significantly, he worked towards reversal of George Edalji's wrongful conviction for maiming horses--a story of both racial bias and animal abuse. Read *Arthur and George* by Julian Barnes. *Adventure of Silver Blaze* was one of the more memorable horse stories in the *Canon*. Dr. Watson was a betting man and "spent almost half his army pension betting on horses."

Behind the Wacker bed

JOHN PETER ALTGELD (1847-1902)--Illinois governor burned in effigy for pardoning the Haymarket "martyrs" who awaited hanging. The popular conception was that the 1896 Haymarket bombers, like the Molly Maguires, were anarchists; this obscured the reality of labor history.

GO WEST, WANDERER

RIGHT BEFORE THE BRIDGE, AT L

EDITH ROCKEFELLER McCORMICK (1872– 1932) was a woman of great wealth and a typical swell of the Golden Age – until the Depression. The daughter of John D. Rockefeller and daughter-in-law of Cyrus McCormick (who also lies in Graceland), Edith at first lived in Council Bluffs, Iowa. She moved to Lake Forest IL and died age 59 of breast cancer. She was a victim of the crash, lavish spending, divorce, and unsound real estate investments.

SHERLOCKIAN NOTE OF NUTTINESS: Edith was into the then-fashionable psychic research and spiritualism. At one party, she represented herself as the wife of King Tut reincarnated.

LUDWIG WOLFF (1836-1911) German immigrant; coppersmith, plumbing and cash register businesses. Like the Hoyts (above), his daughter and grandchildren were killed in the Iroquois fire of 1903. Wolff's underground tomb has a/c--air vents for the afterlife. Rumor is, and it's no wonder, the mausoleum is haunted.

HENRY HARRISON GETTY (1838-1920), Martin Ryerson's partner, lumber merchant, and cemetery neighbor, lies with his wife.

SHERLOCKIAN NOTE: Alternative literary "lumber" usage: *"I consider that a man's brain originally is like a little empty attic, and you have to stock it with such furniture as you choose. A fool takes in all the lumber of every sort that he comes across, so that the knowledge which might be useful to him gets crowded out, or at best is jumbled up with a lot of other things, so that he has a difficulty in laying his hands upon it."* Arthur Conan Doyle.

LOUIS SULLIVAN--Graceland is known as "the cemetery of architects." Sullivan was among the preeminent. He designed the 1890 limestone cube mausoleum in which Henry Harrison Getty lies with his wife. Sullivan died penniless with only his funeral suit. He had been unwilling to design in the Beaux Arts style sweeping the nation after the 1893 Chicago Columbian Exposition and fell out of fashion. His friends paid for the Sullivan tombstone. (see Starrett and Dickens).

DANIEL BURNHAM (1846-1912). Architect and Chicago city planner. Has the best spot--a wooded island accessed by footbridge across Lake Willomere. Stones record the names of the buried residents. Upon his death in 1921, his company was the world's largest architectural firm.

SHERLOCKIAN NOTE: In 1897, Conan Doyle worked with a professional architect in drawing up plans for his Surrey home, Undershaw. It was built complete with stables, a power plant, and environmentally-friendly.

Like President Donald Trump, Conan Doyle also had a hankering for golf. In 1914, on a visit to an army chum in Northern Alberta, Canada, Doyle contributed to the design and layout of a golf course at the Jasper Park Nature Preserve.

JOSEPH MEDILL, (1823-1899) *Chicago Tribune* publisher. Big-time Republican and supporter of Abe Lincoln; strong anti-slaver and abolitionist. Mayor of Chicago after the Great Fire and reconstruction. Like Gov. (Alaska) Sarah Palin, resigned midterm. He lived in Wheaton IL (evangelical town; home of John Birch Society). His former estate, Cantigny, is now open to tours and golfing. His grandson was rightwing Robert McCormick of the *Chicago Tribune*.

SHERLOCKIAN NOTE: Both Joseph Medill and Conan Doyle were honorees of the distinguished New York literary association, the Lotos Club. A Medill grandson was a war correspondent in WWI and wrote cynically about fellow correspondent, Conan Doyle, for having loaned his pen and voice to the Boer War and fomenting terror about the aggressor Hun (Doyle the prescient).

PHILIP DANFORTH ARMOUR (1832-1901). In 1875, with money made in the California gold rush, he arrived to build the world's largest, most pungent slaughterhouse, the Chicago Stockyards. For your reading pleasure, I include my stockyard-related story of "*Gina and Bucca de Beppo*" at the conclusion of this tour book. (Gina is not buried at Graceland.)

SHERLOCKIAN NOTE: Lord St. Simon, in *The Adventure of The Noble Bachelor*, married the daughter of an American from San Francisco who made his pile in the California Gold Rush. In Conan Doyle's time, there were gold rushes aplenty in the U.S., South Africa and in Australia, and the roughest of men made fortunes

ISHAM --the Isham family was of the Isham Lincoln & Beale law firm started by Robert Todd Lincoln (Abe's surviving son) in Chicago and in Springfield.

SHERLOCKIAN NOTE: The 1844 cover of an English issue of sheet music to "the Dark Séance Polka" was illustrated with a picture of Abraham Lincoln holding a candle at a table, with surreally-lit fiddles and tambourines flying above. The caption read "Abraham Lincoln and the Spiritualists." In 1926, Conan Doyle wrote *the History of Spiritualism* in which he claimed Pres. Lincoln engaged a medium who, in a trance, persuaded him to issue the Emancipation Proclamation of 1863. The medium was a friend of Mary Todd Lincoln, a devotee of Spiritualism.

A MIX AND MATCH IN ARCHITECTS CORNER

RODERICK MacARTHUR (1920-1984)-- businessman; founded the Bradford Exchange; pushed his father's foundation to award "genius grants." His tombstone bears the Greek letters for "one foot in fairyland."

SHERLOCKIAN QUERY: what author of Sherlock

Holmes' adventures was himself a fairy enthusiast?

RUTH PAGE (1899-1991) established her namesake theater for the arts in Chicago's near north (a block from the Newberry Library), where the Shakespeare theater once stood before moving to Navy Pier. She was a ballerina and choreographer.

WALTER NETSCH (1920-2008; his father was a VP at Armour) and wife DAWN CLARK NETSCH (1926-2013).

Walter was the architect. Dawn was a brilliant law professor, state senator, solidly pro women's causes, pool and beer. Outspoken about the egregious way in which politicians, starting with Gov. Jim Edgar (under whom she served as Comptroller), spent pension funds--bringing Chicago to the brink today. She urged reporters to "make like Sherlock Holmes" in investigating and reporting facts to the public.

FAZLUR RAHMAN KHAN (1929-1982) Bangladeshi/American, born in the British Raj where he was educated. Came to the U.S. on a Fulbright scholarship, married and became a partner at Skidmore Owens, as architect of the Sears Tower and the John Hancock. Died of a heart attack while working in Saudi Arabia on the Haj Tower. The quotation on his grave marker is in his native Bengali from poet Rabindranath Tagore:

"It marks the beginning for you,
And the end for me.
Together you and me.
That's how life flows."

SHERLOCKIAN NOTE: Bangladesh and Bengal have their troubles. Notwithstanding, the region produces prodigies, as with Fazlur Khan and mystery writer Sharadindu Bandyopadhaya (1899-1970), a contemporary of Conan Doyle's. His stories were of Bengali detectives who investigated in the manner of Sherlock Holmes. Bollywood recently filmed a movie of his famous detective, Byomkesh Bakshi, "truth seeker," set in 1942 Calcutta.

RICHARD NICKEL (1928-1972) photographer, architectural historian and salvage collector. In 1972, many older architectural gems, including Louis Sullivan buildings, were being demolished to make way for trendier buildings. Nickel snuck into the Stock Exchange building, designed by Sullivan, to salvage decorative ornamentals. Two stories of the building fell and crushed him. Nickel's collections are at the Art Institute, various Arts and Architectural clubs, and with the Polish-American Museum (he was of Polish/German descent).

SHERLOCKIAN NOTE: In *the Musgrave Ritual*, Holmes discovers the body of Brunton the butler, entombed beneath the chamber where he thought he would find a Royalist treasure.

ERNIE BANKS (1931-2015). Hall of Fame major league baseball player, beloved by fans. During the time when the Chicago Cubs were particularly terrible, he was an undiminished star. He was cremated and interred at Graceland Cemetery-- a few blocks from Wrigley Field.

CYRUS H. McCORMICK (1809-1884)--A simple headstone marks the grave of the inventor of the wheat reaper, which revolutionized farming, and founder of International Harvester. His dying words were reportedly "work, work, work." His daughter, Anita, who lies beside her parents, was a Spiritualist, lived a good long time, and exchanged correspondence with Arthur Conan Doyle over their common interest in the paranormal.

MARSHALL FIELD (1834-1906). The graveside statue is "Memory." His was the best department store ever. "Give the lady what she wants." If the store didn't have the item requested, they would find it for you. Fields, in its heyday, had a sizable book section where one could find Conan Doyle stories in all varieties and editions. The last few months of Marshall I's life were spent in grief upon the unsolved shooting of his son, Marshall II, in a Chicago brothel. There was a Marshall Field store in horsey Lake Forest IL for many years. In 2008, Marshall V closed the Lake Forest operation and moved away.

MATT RIZZO (1913-1986) "Scorto" is inscribed on his elegant and paradoxical headstone. He became a writer after being blinded in a shooting while robbing a liquor store. He spent 5 1/2 years in Stateville Prison (IL) where he met Nathan Leopold of the 1924 Leopold and Loeb murder case. His papers, such as they are--many on and in braille, are held at the Newberry Library.

43

AND NOW, OUR RETURN TO GRACELAND ROAD AND THE EXIT

CARTER HENRY HARRISON I and II; both were Chicago mayors; the first (1825–1893) was murdered by a disgruntled office seeker: II (1860-1953). A large obelisk marks their resting places. Read *Devil in the White City* by Erik Larson about mayor I, the murderer H.H. Holmes, Daniel Burnham, the city planners and architects, and the 1893 Columbia Exhibition.

SHERLOCKIAN NOTE: In 1915, William Gillette appeared at Essanay Studios in Chicago to shoot the silent Sherlock Holmes film--recently discovered in a

Paris vault and a major entertainment event for Chicago-area Sherlockians. In 1915, Mayor Harrison II's wife appeared in her first film at Essanay, "The Lady of The Shows."

INEZ CLARKE—Graceland myth: In 1880, six-year-old Inez Clarke was struck and killed by a bolt of lightning. Her parents commissioned an artist to create a sculpture in her exact likeness and placed it over her grave. Later, a transparent plexiglass box was added to protect it from the elements. *contra*: The little girl was Inez Briggs who may have died of influenza; her widowed mother remarried John Clarke. The sculptor was Andrew Gagel who, in 1885, sculpted the same figure for a teenage girl in Rosehill Cemetery. At the base of this duplicate statute, he inscribed "Inez."

SHERLOCKIAN NOTE: untangling the web, of course. Elementary!

WALTER LOOMIS NEWBERRY (1804-1868), shipper, dry goods merchant, founder of civic organizations and libraries. The Newberry Library in downtown Chicago is named after him. Outside the library, at leafy Bughouse Square, are held public debates on a variety of topics including civil liberties, Clarence Darrow, and labor rights, with plenty of good-natured heckling. A John Peter Altgeld award is bestowed on the winning debater. My late colleague, criminal defense lawyer Julius Lucius Echeles, was a several-times award winner.

SHERLOCKIAN NOTE: The Newberry hosts annual Conan Doyle seminars and holds an extensive collection of Sherlockian and Conan Doyle papers and includes the memorabilia of the late Dr. Fred Kittle.

AUGUSTUS DICKENS (1827-1866) Younger brother of Charles Dickens; well-educated, heavy drinker, and fated for obscurity. In a migratory divorce, he emigrated to America to escape his wife, Harriette, who was going blind. Augustus brought with him a different woman, Bertha. (Charles Dickens was no better in the respect-for-wives' category). Bertha died of morphine overdose. Augustus worked for the IC railroad. He also appeared in plays based on his brother's writings, entertained Chicago's leading citizens, and otherwise failed in business. Until recently, his Graceland plot was unmarked until the Charles Dickens Society of Chicago purchased a prominent marker.

SHERLOCKIAN NOTE: Dickens was a family friend. Richard Doyle, Conan Doyle's uncle, was a Dickens illustrator. At different times, Conan Doyle and Dickens were members of The Ghost Club— ghostly hauntings, psychic and paranormal phenomena being in vogue. From Dickens' acclaimed debut novel, *The Pickwick Papers*, Dr. Watson declaims about villain Charles Augustus Milverton: "There was something of Mr. Pickwick's benevolence in the appearance marred only by the insincerity of the fixed smile and by the hard glitter of those restless penetrating eyes." (in *The Adventure of Charles Augustus Milverton*).

ABOUT THE AUTHOR

BRENDA ROSSINI, "the Stormy Petrel," is a 35-year member of Chicago-area Sherlockian societies: a Triumvir board member of the Torist International, the board of the Criterion Bar Association and the Scotland Yarders, member of the BeeSpeckled Band of Highwood IL and the Devon Street Beggars of Chicago; attendee and speaker at various and sundry Sherlockian conferences; author of *Sherlockian Ruminations of a Stormy Petrel* (MX Publishers; available at amazon.com); the "Trial of Mycroft Holmes" in *Canadian Holmes*; a welter of Sherlockian toasts; the regularly emailed "Sherlockian Asides" newsletter and the Criterion Bar Association newsletters. Hostess at Chicago-area Sherlockian conventionas during which participants played a personally-created Sherlock Holmes board game. Author and tour guide of the herein *"Graceland Cemetery of Chicago: A Sherlockian Walk Midst the Tombstones."* Reviewer of Sherlockian books and pastiches, whether execrable or commendable, requested or voluntary, at readworthybooks.blogspot.com, in the *Asides,* and at amazon.com. Published as contributor and eyewitness to the *Klinger v. Conan Doyle Ltd. Estate Co.* oral argument published in *I Hear of Sherlock*

Everywhere, www.ihearofsherlock.com/2014/05/an-eyewitness-account-to-free-sherlock.html. Successfully defended Mycroft Holmes in his criminal prosecution, a public proceeding held before judge and jury, with Susan Diamond-Devitt appearing on behalf of the Crown.

BRENDA ROSSINI, agrrtig@aol.com

The Story of Gina

by Brenda Rossini

At the Buca di Beppo restaurant in Oakbrook, IL, there hangs a plaque to one Gina "Bronco" di Bouza who died age 27. Why the plaque? Who was she and why did she die so young?

At age 19, Gina worked at a meatpacking plant in the Chicago Stockyards---where many in the immigrant community found work in the 1950s. She weighed 200 lbs. and was 5 ft. 5 in. tall. A newspaper wrote about her ability to strangle a cow with her thighs.

Billy DeCampo was buyer for an Italian meatpacker...for the company's prosciutto, salami, headcheese, pepperoni, and so forth. That business evolved into the Buca de Beppo restaurants.

Billy talked Gina into pro-wrestling and showmanship. Wrestling was huge in the 1950s: Angelo Poffo, Killer Kowalski, and Gorgeous George among many.

Within a short time, Gina became Women's World Champion Wrestler. She wrestled a woman opponent in a vat of herring on TV, and also had a date with diminutive Sal Mineo.

On Aug. 17, 1957, for a Chicago Stockyards fundraiser, Gina was scheduled to wrestle Bungles, an aged baboon-- brought out of retirement for the event from the calm of his old home at Brookfield Zoo. He had no teeth and his fur had turned grey. The event was billed as the "Battle Royal."

It was a packed house at the Stockyards that evening, with the East Dundee Scots band playing...bagpipes, drums, and clanging brass. The exited crowd shouted and cheered.

Bungles entered the stadium, into the lights and the clamor. He was riding a red tricycle. A banana was hanging on the ropes to draw his attention forward and into the ring. He saw the banana and pedaled his tricycle towards the steps of the ring. His rheumy eyes whirred around the noisy crowd.

As he hoisted himself up the steps, Bungles became agitated and distracted by the tumult. Gina had her back to Bungles. She was walking around the ring, waving to the audience.

Just as Bungles pounced into the ring, and as Gina was waving, and the crowd not yet settled, the East Dundee Scots band struck up their pipes to play the national anthem.

To this tune, and to the din, Old Bungles rushed towards Gina. Without provocation, Bungles picked her up, lifted her high, and with his strong baboon paws, in an instant snapped her neck, twirled her body, and then sent it flying into the panic-stricken, horrified crowd. Gina was dead.

In a frenzy, Bungles began feverishly chewing on the ring ropes. Police officers on crowd control promptly dispatched him and shot him dead. Thus ended Bungles' short but eventful retirement.

And thus ends the story of Gina "Bronco" di Bouza and her ring career.

Also from MX Publishing

MX Publishing is the world's largest specialist Sherlock Holmes publisher, with over a hundred titles and fifty authors creating the latest in Sherlock Holmes fiction and non-fiction.

From traditional short stories and novels to travel guides and quiz books, MX Publishing cater for all Holmes fans.

The collection includes leading titles such as _Benedict Cumberbatch In Transition_ and _The Norwood Author_ which won the 2011 Howlett Award (Sherlock Holmes Book of the Year).

MX Publishing also has one of the largest communities of Holmes fans on Facebook with regular contributions from dozens of authors.

www.mxpublishing.com

Also from MX Publishing

The Missing Authors Series

Sherlock Holmes and The Adventure of The Grinning Cat
Sherlock Holmes and The Nautilus Adventure
Sherlock Holmes and The Round Table Adventure

"Joseph Svec, III is brilliant in entwining two endearing and enduring classics of literature, blending the factual with the fantastical; the playful with the pensive; and the mischievous with the mysterious. We shall, all of us young and old, benefit with a cup of tea, a tranquil afternoon, and a copy of Sherlock Holmes, The Adventure of the Grinning Cat."
Amador County Holmes Hounds Sherlockian Society

www.mxpublishing.com

Also from MX Publishing

The American Literati Series

The Final Page of Baker Street
The Baron of Brede Place
Seventeen Minutes To Baker Street

"The really amazing thing about this book is the author's ability to call up the 'essence' of both the Baker Street 'digs' of Holmes and Watson as well as that of the 'mean streets' of Marlowe's Los Angeles. Although none of the action takes place in either place, Holmes and Watson share a sense of camaraderie and self-confidence in facing threats and problems that also pervades many of the later tales in the Canon. Following their conversations and banter is a return to Edwardian England and its certainties and hope for the future. This is definitely the world before The Great War."
Philip K Jones

www.mxpublishing.com

Also from MX Publishing

The Detective and The Woman Series

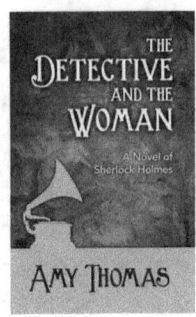  

The Detective and The Woman
The Detective, The Woman and The Winking Tree
The Detective, The Woman and The Silent Hive

"The book is entertaining, puzzling and a lot of fun. I believe the author has hit on the only type of long-term relationship possible for Sherlock Holmes and Irene Adler. The details of the narrative only add force to the romantic defects we expect in both of them and their growth and development are truly marvelous to watch. This is not a love story. Instead, it is a coming-of-age tale starring two of our favorite characters."
Philip K Jones

www.mxpublishing.com

Also from MX Publishing

The Sherlock Holmes and Enoch Hale Series

The Amateur Executioner
The Poisoned Penman
The Egyptian Curse

"The Amateur Executioner: Enoch Hale Meets Sherlock Holmes", the first collaboration between Dan Andriacco and Kieran McMullen, concerns the possibility of a Fenian attack in London. Hale, a native Bostonian, is a reporter for London's Central News Syndicate - where, in 1920, Horace Harker is still a familiar figure, though far from revered. "The Amateur Executioner" takes us into an ambiguous and murky world where right and wrong aren't always distinguishable. I look forward to reading more about Enoch Hale."
Sherlock Holmes Society of London

www.mxpublishing.com

www.ingramcontent.com/pod-product-compliance
Lightning Source LLC
Chambersburg PA
CBHW071349130626
46556CB00005B/2100